My Gramma
Has Ants in
Her Pants

Paula Moyer Savaiano

Paula Moyer Savaiano
LeClaire, Iowa

WestBow Press books may be ordered through booksellers or by contacting:

WestBow Press
A Division of Thomas Nelson & Zondervan
1663 Liberty Drive
Bloomington, IN 47403
www.westbowpress.com
1 (866) 928-1240

Because of the dynamic nature of the Internet, any web addresses or links contained in this book may have changed
since publication and may no longer be valid. The views expressed in this work are solely those of the author and do
not necessarily reflect the views of the publisher, and the publisher hereby disclaims any responsibility for them.

Any people depicted in stock imagery provided by Thinkstock are models,
and such images are being used for illustrative purposes only.
Certain stock imagery © Thinkstock.

ISBN: 978-1-5127-3746-2 (sc)
ISBN: 978-1-5127-3747-9 (e)

Library of Congress Control Number: 2016905650

Print information available on the last page.

WestBow Press rev. date: 06/14/2016

WESTBOW
PRESS®
A DIVISION OF THOMAS NELSON
& ZONDERVAN

My Gramma Stories are inspired by and dedicated to my mother, Jeanne Moyer, who is both GRAMMA to 7 and GREAT GRAMMA to 15. She is young at heart, full of energy, and always ready for FUN!

My gramma and I were out hikin', ya know,

High in the mountains of Colorado.

We were walkin' along admirin' the view~

The clear streams, tall pines, and the sky oh so blue.

We were mindin' our business, just marchin' along

Singin' a little ditty, a hikin' song.

It went like this; join in if you'd like.

    Right, left — Left, right

    Lift those legs up.

    Hike, hike, hike!

We stayed on the path and kept to the beat.

Good thing Gramma had sneakers on her feet.

We hiked and hiked 'til half past noon.

We were gettin' the hungries; we had to eat soon.

So we sat for a spell on an old hollow log.

Not far, Bullfrog croaked in his bog.

While Gramma was sittin', she was rubbin' her belly.

"My favorite, yum, yum — peanut butter and jelly."

Just as she was ready to take her first bite,

She jumped to her feet; it was quite a sight.

She ran in a circle, then hopped up and down.

She wiggled and jiggled; she looked like a clown.

"Gramma, oh Gramma, what's happened to you?"

She said, "Oh Honey, I haven't a clue."

But as I approached that old hollow log,

I heard the croak of that big bullfrog.

He said, "Your gramma's got ants in her pants,

And that's why she's doin' the hootchy kootchy dance."

Those little red ants were mad as could be

'Cause Gramma had invaded their privacy.

They crawled up her bloomers and gave her a bite.

Gramma ran for the bushes 'til she was out of sight.

She took off those bloomers and gave 'em a shake.

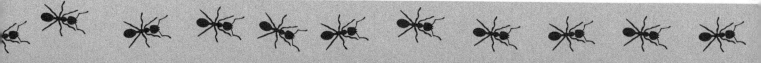

Then my gramma jumped right into the lake.

And when she came out, we were waitin' there.

"Oh Gramma, you gave us quite a scare."

The frog in the bog had a little advice.

"Gramma," he croaked, "you're oh so nice.

But don't ya know jelly is sweet.

Those ants were just waitin' for a special treat."

And with that Bullfrog took one big leap.

He promised my gramma her secret he'd keep.

From that day on, as we marched along,

Gramma was singin' a new hikin' song.

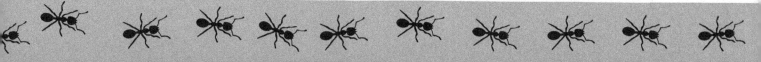

It went like this; join in if you'd like.

> Right, left – Left, right
>
> Lift those legs up.
>
> Hike, hike, hike!
>
> No more ants in my pants.
>
> No more hootchy kootchy dance.
>
> No more lunch on the log.
>
> So long, Froggie in the bog.

THE END

CPSIA information can be obtained
at www.ICGtesting.com
Printed in the USA
BVOW05s1423040517
483155BV00006B/9/P

9 781512 737462